MONSTER HIGH

DIARIES

MONSTER HIGH™

DIARIES

CLAWDEEN WOLF
AND THE FREAKY-FABULOUS
FASHION SHOW

By Nessi Monstrata

LITTLE, BROWN AND COMPANY
New York Boston

Copyright © 2016 by Mattel, Inc. All rights reserved. MONSTER HIGH and
associated trademarks are owned by and used under license from Mattel, Inc.

Little, Brown and Company

Hachette Book Group
1290 Avenue of the Americas, New York, NY 10104
Visit us at lb-kids.com

Little, Brown and Company is a division of Hachette Book Group, Inc.
The Little, Brown name and logo are trademarks of Hachette Book Group, Inc.

The publisher is not responsible for websites (or their content)
that are not owned by the publisher.

First Edition: May 2016

[CIP to come]

ISBN 978-0-316-30078-0

10 9 8 7 6 5 4 3 2 1

RRD-C

Printed in the United States of America

Diary Entry

I'm monstrously good at most things, but... honestly? Keeping a diary is so not one of them. I'm going to stick to it this time, and here's why: I'm getting ready to stage a major fashion show! There's SO much to do to get ready, and I read on one of my fashion blogs that some of my favorite designers use their sketchbooks for more than just sketching—they use them to keep track of all the details associated with launching a new collection. I don't like the idea of mixing my words with my sketches, so I will keep those separate, but I'm going to give this diary thing a try and see if it helps keep me organized and on track.

❀ 1 ❀

It's so important that everything goes smoothly with this show. Why? Well, I guess I should write down my reasons for putting on this show, since I'm supposed to keep notes about everything in this diary. Here goes...

It all started a few weeks ago when I was howling to my brother, Clawd, about how the Fearleading squad uniforms at Monster High could really use an update. (They're so last scaremester!) Then, while he and I were out tossing around a ball at the park, we both started growling about how Monster High is in serious need of some new sports equipment—some of the balls we use in gym class are older than the de Nile family estate!

Clawd told me if I felt so passionately about the squad uniforms and the school sports equipment, I should do something about it. I realized he was totally right! An entrepreneur (like me!) finds opportunities and goes after them. So after I talked to Headless Headmistress Bloodgood and learned there was no extra money in the budget for either new uniforms or equipment, I realized I was going to have to find some way to raise the money to make things right myself.

I spent a few nights brainstorming fund-raising ideas with my pack of ghoulfriends—Frankie Stein is totally clawesome at coming up with ways to bring ideas to life, since she's the daughter of an inventor, and Draculaura has a creeperific imagination—and that's when we decided it would be fangtastic if I could host a fashion show to help raise money for Monster High. I'll be able to sell some of the fiercest pieces after the show, and we'll charge admission to the show itself. I've done some rough calculations, and if my figures are correct, we should make enough to get all new uniforms for the Fearleading team AND a bunch of new balls and nets and whatever else we need to make the Monster High gym fangtastic.

Now that planning is under way, I can tell it's going to be creeperific! For the past few weeks,

I've been sketching up a ton of new designs and working with my ghouls to plan some of the show details. There are so many things to keep straight, but my ghoulfriends have been a huge help. I couldn't do this without them!

Then, last weekend, while we were fanging at the Maul checking out the new summer collection at Neiman Monstrous, my BFF Draculaura bought me this scary-cute notebook. She suggested I jot down a few notes every day that will help me keep a record of my progress between now and the night of the show. That reminded me of what I'd read on the fashion blog, and another lightbulb went off in my head, and there you have it: my new diary!

Since I'm building my own fashion empire, it's extra important that I learn from any problems and tangles I encounter. I'm not the kind of ghoul who likes to make the same mistake twice! So there... the first entry in Clawdeen Wolf's freaky-fabulous fashion diary.

NOTE: This is a PRIVATE diary.

To my pack (that means you, especially, Howleen):
You better not be reading this, or I'm swapping
your steak for one of Draculaura's tofu dogs.
Fair warning!

Clawdeen

CHAPTER ONE

*T**icktock.***

Ticktock.

Ticktock.

Clawdeen Wolf glanced up at the enormous grandfather clock perched against the wall of her Monster High economics classroom and sighed. Life usually moved at the speed of moonlight for the fashionable werewolf. But today—the last day of school before summer scarecation—time was totally dragging.

With only thirty-six minutes left until break began, Clawdeen was having a hard time thinking about anything other than relaxing with her ghoulfriends, long afternoon runs, baseball games, and—most important—endless hours to work on her newest fashion designs.

Most days, Clawdeen loved economics. As a talented designer with a dream of one day running her own fashion empire, Clawdeen knew how important it was for her to learn about the business of design. Even though her favorite part of fashion was the sketching and stitching, the fiercely independent werewolf never wanted to have to rely on other people to run her business for her. She intended to manage every aspect of her future empire, thank you very much.

But today, it was hard to focus on economics when there were so many other things on her mind.

Ticktock.

Ticktock.

Clawdeen tried her best to pay careful attention to the lecture, but after a few moments, she gave up and stifled a yawn. Her head just wasn't in the economics game. She thought about it and decided that she'd learned so much in class already this year, maybe letting her mind wander just a little bit during the last few minutes of the last class of the day wouldn't be terrible. Fifteen minutes to go, and then she could dedicate every minute of the next two weeks to her Freaky-Fabulous Fashion Show.

She turned to a fresh page in her notebook and began to doodle. She tried to only sketch designs in her special design sketchbook, but because inspiration struck at any moment, almost all of Clawdeen's school notebooks ended up filled with fashion sketches eventually.

As she leaned over her work, letting her creative instincts take over, Clawdeen's soft, wavy brown hair cascaded past her shoulders. Her curls created a thick curtain around her desk. She bit her lower lip and focused, watching as a fabulous dress began to take shape on the page. Living in a small house with a huge pack, Clawdeen rarely got time to focus on her sketches without someone interrupting her work. These few minutes of alone time were precious, and Clawdeen wasn't going to let them go to waste. She bent her head over the page and let the inspiration flow from her fingers.

As her pencil drew lines and curves, Clawdeen could see the dress she was putting on the page turning into something real. She pictured black satin embellishments on the bodice and a gold lining with the tiniest hint of purple peeking out of the neckline...or maybe the other way around? Purple lining with a gold accent? She would have to figure that out later. For now, it was all about shape. After a moment's consideration, she scrubbed her eraser over the sleeves of the dress, turning it into a sleeveless design with a quick flick of her pencil.

Clawdeen grinned. *Perfect.* She closed her eyes, imagining the dress floating across the stage during a fashion show in front of hundreds—thousands!—of adoring fans. Monsters would be lined up around the block for a chance to buy the dress. All the stores would beg her to sell it as an exclusive. Clawdeen would be known around the world as the fashionista who had designed the dress of the century.

She opened her eyes again and cocked her head to the side. Studying the dress more carefully, she suddenly realized her ghoulfriend Frankie Stein, the daughter of Frankenstein, would look totally voltageous in this design. With its electric rawness, it was as if the dress had been designed just for her! Clawdeen must have had Frankie in the back of her mind as she sketched. She suddenly decided that even if every store in the Maul begged her for the right to sell it, Clawdeen would only make one copy of this particular design, and she'd give it to her ghoulfriend. She loved working up special pieces for the monsters she loved, outfits that were as unique and one of a kind as each of her ghoulfriends.

Just as Clawdeen was putting the finishing touches on the sketch of Frankie's dress, someone bumped into her from behind. Her pencil scratched across the page. "Hey, watch it!" Clawdeen snapped, slamming the notebook closed. She flicked her gaze up and growled at Deuce Gorgon, who was racing past her toward the door of the classroom. She glared at him, annoyed that he had interrupted her design time.

"Catnap's over, Clawdeen—school's out for the summer!" Deuce called over his shoulder. With a wink, he bolted into the hallway.

Clawdeen looked around. Sure enough, the classroom was already half empty. It always amazed her how quickly time flew by when she was working on designs! Clawdeen swiped a fresh coat of gloss across her lips, stuffed her books and pencils into her bag, and headed out into the packed Monster High hallway.

"What's up, ghouls?" she called to Frankie and Draculaura, the daughter of Dracula. Two of Clawdeen's closest ghoulfriends were gathered together near Frankie's locker, waiting for Cleo de Nile and Lagoona Blue to join them. Clawdeen hustled to snag the last of her things from her locker—a sparkle-studded mirror, a messy stack of loose sketches, and at least a dozen tubes of lip gloss—and made her way toward the waiting pack. "Are we still on for this afternoon?" she asked, linking arms with Frankie and Draculaura as she walked up to them. "Everyone want to fang out at my place after school to celebrate the end of the year with some ice scream? We can talk about the Freaky-Fabulous Fashion Show!

I'd love to see what fun designs you ghouls have come up with to add to the collection."

Because Clawdeen's upcoming fashion show was a fund-raiser for Monster High, she had enlisted the help of her ghoulfriends to design some of the pieces that would be featured in the show. Though most of the show would be made up of Clawdeen's signature designs, she also wanted to highlight her best ghoulfriends' freaky fashions. With a few friend-designed pieces, the show would represent the true variety of personalities and styles at Monster High. And not only were they serving as guest designers, but the Monster High ghouls would be walking as models in the show too. Clawdeen knew that with her pack of ghouls involved in such an important way, the show would truly represent her as a designer. After all, her ghoulfriends were a source of inspiration to her, and their friendship was a huge part of who she was.

"I'm definitely up for screechza," Frankie said, rubbing her stomach. Frankie was *always* up for screechza. "But I hope you're not expecting me to come up with any dress designs. I think it would be totally voltageous to help out with set design or something like that, but the actual fashion design is probably best left to the experts." Frankie pulled her black-and-white-striped hair into a ponytail and waved at some of their other classmates. She was the friendliest ghoul Clawdeen knew. "See you next scaremester!" Frankie said, waving at everyone who passed. "Have a great summer scarecation!"

"If you don't want to design a piece of clothing, no biggie," Clawdeen said. "But I'm happy to help you out if you change your mind. We can work on something together. A freaky fusion of my design and your style? We could really rock a look. What do you say?"

Frankie laughed. "Thanks, Clawdeen. But I'm

much more comfortable working on my own kind of creations in the lab. I think I'll stick to that for now. But I would love to model one of your designs on the runway, if you'll still let me!" Under her breath, she muttered, "Let's just hope I don't lose my stitches...."

"You'll be great," Clawdeen promised. "And I'd love to have your help with set design." Clawdeen respected her friend's decision, but she couldn't imagine not wanting to design something! That and sports kept her blood pumping. At that moment, her whole body was buzzing with excitement. She couldn't wait to get to work on the piece she'd sketched during economics. Frankie was going to love it! It would be the perfect piece for her to wear during the Freaky-Fabulous Fashion Show!

"I'm totally in," Cleo added. "Did I tell you? I've already posted a few of my sketches online. I set up a poll so my fans can vote for their faves.

I also sent the designs over to my close, personal ghoulfriend—Doomatella Verscarce—and she's going to get back to me with her thoughts next week." She flicked her long, shiny hair over her shoulder and smiled contentedly.

"That's great, Cleo," Clawdeen said. Clawdeen had a feeling the Egyptian princess's design would be more than a little over-the-top once she got feedback from that many people. But over-the-top suited Cleo. "I can't wait to see what you've come up with."

As Frankie and the other ghouls bid their classmates farewell for the summer howlidays, Draculaura stood on tiptoes in her platform heels and scanned the hallways looking for her boyfriend, Clawd. "Where's my sweetie?" the petite vampire crooned. Her pink-streaked black hair swished from side to side as she looked up and down the hallways for any sign of Clawdeen's brother. "I want to say good-bye before we leave school. It's going to be so hard not seeing him every hour during summer break."

Clawdeen laughed and rolled her eyes playfully. Draculaura and Clawd were practically inseparable. Even though Draculaura was a vampire and Clawdeen's family were werewolves, all the Wolfs considered Draculaura to be part of their pack. Given that she was beast friends with Clawdeen *and* Clawd's ghoulfriend, Draculaura was practically a member of their family. "Ghoul, chill. You'll see him back at my place later," Clawdeen reminded Draculaura. "He lives with me, remember?"

Draculaura's already-pinkish skin flushed a deeper crimson. "Uh, yeah, I *know*! I just wanted to say good-bye—" Suddenly, her face split into a huge smile. Clawd had appeared around the corner, holding a Casketball under his arm. "Oh, look, there he is! Clawd, sweetie, over here!"

Clawd sauntered over and spun Draculaura around and around in a big hug. She rubbed his ears playfully. "Do you want to come over after school?" he asked Draculaura. "A few of us are getting together in our yard to throw around a ball and grill up some food."

Clawdeen glared at him. "What do you mean 'a few of us'? And where exactly are you getting together?"

"A few of the guys from the Casketball team," Clawd said, shrugging. Under his breath, he added, "Or more like the *whole* Casketball team. At our house. Dad said it was okay when I asked him this morning...."

"Well, Mom said *I* could have friends over after school," Clawdeen said, clearly exasperated. "The ghouls and I are getting together to work on designs for my show."

"It'll be a full house, then," Clawd replied sheepishly.

Clawdeen shot him a look, obviously annoyed.

Just then, Clawd and Clawdeen's younger sister, Howleen, came tearing around the corner with a pack of her friends. "Smell you at home, sis!" she called out to Clawdeen. "Dibs on our room this afternoon! My friends and I are watching boo-vies!"

Clawdeen held up one manicured hand. "Hold on, Howleen. You can't call dibs on our room. It's *our* room. We share it, remember?" She narrowed her eyes at her little sister and added, "And what do you mean 'watching boo-vies'?"

"Boo-vies?" Howleen said slowly. "Boo-vies... you know, those fun little videos with famous Hauntlywood actors and actresses? They're stories written by screamwriters, and you watch them on TV or at the theater...." Howleen cracked herself up. Behind her, her friends giggled. "Sound familiar?"

Clawdeen growled at her sister. "Really cute, Howleen. You're hilarious. What's not cute is *you* bringing your friends home when I'm already bringing my friends home. We were going to fang out in my room."

"*Our* room," Howleen corrected. "And feel free to fang out in there, as long as you don't mind fanging out with me and my ghoulfriends. We don't mind squishing in."

Clawdeen glared at her sister, then her brother. "We can't *all* have friends over."

"Dad said it was okay," Howleen argued back.

Clawd shrugged. "Why can't we? The more the merrier. Catch you at home," he said, tossing the Casketball in the air.

Clawdeen caught it and threw it back at him. "Ugh!" As Howleen and Clawd walked away, Clawdeen spun around and let out a loud, huffy sigh. "They drive me crazy!" she said to her ghoulfriends.

Frankie, Draculaura, Cleo, and Lagoona all stared back at her.

"Well, it sounds like it will definitely be a full house, like Clawd said, but maybe we can find fashion inspiration in all the chaos," Draculaura said finally.

Lagoona nodded, running her fingers through her long blue-blond hair. The laid-back daughter of a sea monster was great at giving advice just when her friends needed it. "Yeah, we'll just make the most of it, Clawdeen. It's no big deal. Besides…they're your pack. Believe me, I know it can be tough to have to share your house with so many siblings, but they are as entitled to have friends over as you are.…"

"I guess maybe you're right," Clawdeen said after a minute.

"Phew, I'm glad you're not mad anymore!" Frankie said, a smile lighting up her face. "I hate when you fight with your siblings! You're so lucky to have them. I *wish* I had siblings!"

"Fight?" Clawdeen laughed. "That wasn't a fight!"

"It wasn't?" Draculaura asked slowly. Growing up with Dracula for a father, Draculaura was used to a different family dynamic. She and her father discussed everything very calmly. She could never get used to the way Clawdeen and her siblings shouted at one another. They all had a tendency to say whatever was on their minds and often at a very loud decibel.

"Nah." Clawdeen shrugged. "That was nothing. You know we bicker like that all the time. And you're right, Frankie. I'm totally lucky to have them. As much as they bug me, I love my siblings…just like I love you ghouls!"

All the ghouls looked relieved to hear that they weren't in the middle of a Wolf family war.

"We fight because we love one another. If I didn't like them, I wouldn't bother," Clawdeen explained. "But bickering is what we do. It's kind of our thing." She laughed, and the other girls joined her. "Now, come on—if we want to have any chance of getting the cookies my mom baked last night, we'd better hurry. Between Howleen's pack, Clawd's pack, and all of us, it sounds like most of Monster High is gathering at my house. Let's move it, ghouls! Cookies and screechza, coming right up!"

Diary Entry

I love my family like crazy. Of course, they sometimes drive me crazy too—doesn't everyone's pack? But no matter how much they make my fur stand on end on an almost-daily basis, they truly mean the world to me.

Do I ever wish I could live in a house where I didn't have to share the hot water every morning? Totally.

Do I love the days when I wake up first and get to shower and shave (and sometimes shave again) before Clawd clogs the drain with his shedding issues? For sure.

Would it be great to have my own bedroom so I wouldn't have to worry about Howleen absentmindedly chewing the sleeve off my best leather jacket while she reads? Absolutely.

But being a part of my pack is (almost always) worth all the little inconveniences that come with a big family. Sure, it would be nice to be able to stretch out and have a little more space from time to time, but I really do think our house is cozy, loving, and fun. And we all look out for one another, which is a majorly clawesome perk of wolf culture.

Summer at our house gets even crazier. My big sis, Clawdia, comes home from Londoom for a few months, and we always have a rotating group of family guests—cousins, aunts, uncles, grandwolves (though thankfully not all at the same time!). Knowing how chaotic things can be in the summer at the Wolf house, it's going to be extra tricky to find time to get everything ready for the Freaky-Fabulous Fashion Show this year.

So I guess that's what I'm writing about in my diary today. I only have two weeks left to get everything done, and about two years' worth of work to do. The good news is, with school out for the summer, I can work full-time on the show. Hopefully, I can kick Howleen out of our room for a while every day to get some work done. Believe me, I'm going to need every last second.

This show is so important to me, and because so much is riding on it, I want to get it right. Especially since my ghoulfriends have been giving up so much of their free time to help me out. I want to prove to them—and myself—that I can successfully manage a fashion show! This is a perfect chance to prove I can run my own fashion empire someday.

Enough writing about what I'm doing... time to get back to work. These designs aren't going to sew themselves.

NOTE: This is a PRIVATE diary. To anyone who might be sniffing around inside these pages (that's YOU, Howleen): Read this, and I'm sneaking boiled spinach into your breakfast scramble. Keep out!

Clawdeen

CHAPTER TWO

With summer break officially under way, Clawdeen was thrilled she finally had unlimited time to work on her pieces for the Freaky-Fabulous Fashion Show. During the last two weeks of school, she had really only had time to sketch ideas. She would squeeze in some design time between classes or after studying for finals, but it was hard to find the time to cut and sew with so many end-of-the-year activities.

Now that she had all day to work, she'd finally gotten to start cutting and stitching up some of her favorite pieces.

"Hold still," she told Draculaura, clutching a pin between her lips. Frankie and Draculaura had come over to fang out for the afternoon, and Clawdeen was using this opportunity to fit them for the dresses they would be wearing in the show. None of the pieces were done yet, but Clawdeen couldn't wait to see what they were going to look like on her real-life models. Clawdeen carefully pressed the pin into the soft fabric.

Draculaura craned her head around, trying to get a look at her dress in the mirror. Of course, being a vampire, she couldn't see her face in the mirror. "Ouch!" Draculaura cried when the pin pricked her upper arm. Her eyes watered, and she rubbed her tender skin. Draculaura averted her eyes—she always got woozy at the sight of blood. "I know I have sharp fangs, but I still don't love the feeling of being stabbed with your sewing tools. I'm not a pincushion, you know."

"Sorry," Clawdeen said, gently rubbing her friend's shoulder where she had pricked her. Clawdeen felt bad for poking her. "But I did tell you to hold still."

The cut of the dress was absolutely perfect for Draculaura's petite frame. The gown looked totally elegant, and Draculaura sucked in a breath. "Wait!" Clawdeen said, reaching under the sheet she'd been using to protect her half-done pieces to grab something small and round. Though it was still unfinished, Clawdeen had begun to assemble a little clutch purse that would serve as the perfect accessory for the dress.

"So what do you think?" Draculaura said when Clawdeen stepped back. Draculaura spun around, and all three girls gazed at the dress in the mirror on Howleen's side of the bedroom. Draculaura let out a tiny gasp, Frankie stared, and Clawdeen felt a huge wave of relief wash over her.

"It's totes amazing," Draculaura said, looking down at the dress. She couldn't see herself in the mirror, but the dress *felt* so great that Draculaura knew it looked fangulous.

"Wow," Frankie murmured. "Clawdeen, this is one of the best designs you've ever done. I love the detail along the bottom of the skirt. So voltageous."

"I know! I'm thrilled with how it's coming along!" Clawdeen said happily. "Wait until you see your outfit, Frankie. You're going to freak."

Clawdeen still had a lot of work to do, but now that she could see how clawesome the dress would look when it was finished, she was motivated to work even harder on the rest of her collection. Her hope was that it would represent her as a designer but also suit the personality and style of each of her models. She wanted this show to scream Monster High—and highlight each of her ghoulfriends' freaky and fabulous personalities! Every piece had to be as unique and as special as her friends were.

"I can't believe you actually made that dress," Frankie said, settling in on Clawdeen's bed. The bedroom Clawdeen shared with Howleen was so tiny that the only free space to fang out was on the beds. "It's totally electrifying."

"And I can't believe *you* can build your very own pets in your lab," Clawdeen said admiringly. "We all have our strengths. Yours is inventing and building; mine just happens to be design." She shrugged.

Frankie stood up and stepped on the crate Clawdeen had set next to her bed, readying herself for her own fitting. For the past few weeks,

Clawdeen had been extra careful to keep all her sewing supplies on her own side of the room—she didn't want to risk Howleen pawing through her stuff. Clawdeen had even gone so far as to draw a line down the center of the room with a strip of hem tape. Not that it would keep Howleen out of her side of the room—their shared bedroom was so tight and jam-packed with two ghouls' stuff that Howleen often had to hop up and over the end of Clawdeen's bed to get into the room. But Clawdeen hoped the tape would serve as a reminder to her sister to be careful with all the fashion show materials. The tape created a dividing line, even though there really was no such thing as personal boundaries in the Wolf house.

Clawdeen stepped over to the clothing rack she had set up near the foot of her bed. She lifted the sheet and picked up Frankie's outfit.

"Ooh!" Frankie cheered. "Blue!"

"Of course," Clawdeen told her. "Nothing but the best for you, right, ghoul?"

The dress still had a long way to go before it was done, but Clawdeen could already tell it was going to be a showstopper. The whole dress was made out of black and white satin, with a bold blue underskirt that was visible when Frankie moved her body to and fro. The bodice was fitted, and the skirt swished out in an angled swoop. Little bits of gold lace peeked out of the neckline, and Clawdeen had sewn a tiny strip of the same gold lace along the bottom hem. The piece was exciting and fun, just like Frankie.

Clawdeen was overcome with pride and happiness. She and Frankie smiled at each other in the mirror. "I *love* it!" Frankie gushed. "It's so *me*. It's electrifying, Clawdeen! Thank you."

There was a knock at the door, and a moment later, Clawd poked his head into the room.

"Wow!" he said when he saw Draculaura. "Did you design that, sis?"

Clawdeen beamed. "I sure did. So what do you think? Gore-geous, right?"

"The ghoul and the dress are both incredible," Clawd crooned.

"Aw," Draculaura said, blushing. "Thanks, sweetie." She moved toward Clawd, but Clawdeen stopped her.

"No hugs right now," she said, holding her arm out to stop Clawd from coming any farther into the room. "Don't take another step! I don't want fur all over my designs."

"Just *one* hug?" Clawd begged. He waved his arms around in the door of Clawdeen's bedroom, sprinkling hairs all over Clawdeen's bedspread.

"Just one hug and I'll be lint-rolling this dress for the next two weeks," Clawdeen warned. "Hands off the models!"

Clawd laughed. "Got anything for me to try on yet?"

Clawdeen shook her head. She had promised to include Clawd and Howleen in the show too, since they were such an important part of her "brand." The night after she'd told Howleen she would get to walk in the show, she had caught her sister peeking at the pieces she'd been trying so hard to keep hidden. She knew Howleen had tried on at least one of the dresses—a shimmery aqua one she had set aside for Lagoona—since her extra-sensitive sense of smell picked up the scent of her little sis on the dress. "I'm not done with your outfit yet. I'm working on a clawe-some green suit for you to wear in the show, but I haven't even cut it out. Hopefully, I can size you tomorrow."

Clawd nodded. "Right on. I can model it for Great-Great-Great-Grandwolf then. And the cousins."

Clawdeen stared at her brother. "Huh?"

"When they get here tomorrow," Clawd said with a shrug. He cocked his head and said slowly, "You do know the whole family is coming tomorrow...right?"

"The *whole* family?" Clawdeen said, gulping. Their pack was huge. "What do you mean, the whole family?"

"Twenty-five of our family members are rolling in tomorrow," Clawd said. "Gran, Great-Gran, Great-Great-Gran, Great-Great-Great-Gran, and Great-Great-Great-Grandwolf, all of Mom's sisters, Cousin Clawdette, and the quadruplets..." Clawd trailed off, noticing Clawdeen's look of horror. "Mom and Dad haven't mentioned it yet? Last-minute family reunion. They're all staying here. For two weeks."

Clawdeen shook her head. *Two weeks.* Though she loved her family, when they came to visit, life got even crazier than usual. Kids everywhere, sleeping bags tossed down in every free corner, family dinners every night. "B-but—" she stammered. "But if they're staying here"—she closed her eyes and took a deep breath—"how will I finish my designs? I won't have time or space to work! My Freaky-Fabulous Fashion Show will be a freaky fashion disaster!"

Draculaura and Frankie exchanged a nervous look. "We can help..." Draculaura said. But Clawdeen was so upset, she was barely listening.

"Pack first," Clawd reminded his sister. "Those are the rules, remember?" He shot Clawdeen a sympathetic smile, then headed back out into the hall. "Don't worry, sis. You'll figure it out. You always do."

Clawdeen flopped onto her bed and groaned. Clawd was right—pack rules dictated that family came first and was the most important thing. Family first, always and forever. But the fashion show was also really important to her. She had so much to do and less than two weeks left to get it all done!

Their house was already crowded and crazy with just her immediate family…throw in a bunch of grans, a litter of cousins, and a pack of chattering aunties, and the next two weeks were about to get a *lot* more tangled.

Diary Entry

Here's what you need to know about my pack: It's huge. And loud. And fun.

But sometimes, when the whole pack is jammed together, it's hard to have any time to myself. When I'm at Monster High or fanging out with my ghoulfriends, I feel like I can do my own thing when I want to. Like an individual. But when the whole Wolf clan gathers, I become just one wolf in a huge pack. Like I can't do my own independent thing, you know? We blend together into this giant furry ball of claws and fangs and stories that are all really similar. Everyone's unique personalities get squeezed into the bigger pack and become the "pack identity." It's a great feeling to have so many loved ones around you, but with everything I have to get done for the fashion show, I just don't know how I can make them understand that this wolf needs some alone time.

Traditional werewolf culture can be a little hard for me and Clawd and Howleen to deal with because we're used to mixing with a more blended group in school. We're not just part of the pack when we're at school. One of the reasons I love my Monster High family so much is that we're all really different and unique—and we're all an important part of the group. We're our own monsters, and everyone knows us as Clawdeen or Clawd or Howleen—the individuals. Not just another member of the clan. At home, there's an expectation that I identify as a Wolf first, Clawdeen second.

The other thing that can be hard about having our bigger pack around is that my ghoulfriends can't really fang out over at my place as much. My parents don't mind all our other friends fanging around with us at school—or coming over after school, as long as we clean up after ourselves—but when the whole pack is here, we're expected to drop our Monster High friends and totally focus on the family.

Pack first, everything and everyone else a distant thirteenth.

Anyone who knows me knows I don't like being told what to do. So it can be <u>hard to follow</u> the pack rules. Sometimes I feel confined by all the family expectations and rules. And these next two weeks? It's going to be impossible to follow the pack-first rule. My Freaky-Fabulous Fashion Show has to come first—I committed to it, and it's like my future is hanging in the balance. But the question is, will my pack understand that I have to put them second?

NOTE: This is a PRIVATE diary. Paws off! And if someone is reading this, you better not forget that my designs for the fashion show are totally

OFF-LIMITS. I know someone (ahem, Howleen) has been sniffing around my side of the room. I'm going to howl if you don't back off and quit trying them on before they're ready. I need some space to create in private, or this show is going to be a fashion disaster!

Clawdeen

CHAPTER THREE

H ey, Mom!" Clawdeen shouted over the sound of the vacuum cleaner. "Mom!"

Clawdeen's mom switched off the vacuum cleaner and pulled her earbuds out of her ears. She always listened to music when she vacuumed, dancing around with the vacuum. She said it made the tedious job fun. One of the things Clawdeen loved most about her family was their ability to turn anything from an annoying task or a difficult situation into something positive.

"Filter's clogged again," her mom told her, sighing. "Too much hair."

"Sorry, Mom," Clawdeen said, tossing her huge sewing bag over one shoulder. That morning, she had packed up all her sketchbooks and a few of her key pieces that were cut but not yet sewn. Finding and pulling everything together had taken *ages*, since Howleen had left their bedroom a total mess! Clawdeen often fantasized about having a sewing room of her very own, where she could keep everything safe in its place and know no one other than her would ever touch or move it. When she opened her own business, she would make sure to have at least one sewing room at home, plus one at the office. Now, under the awkward weight of the bag, Clawdeen teetered for a moment on her platform boots. Then she righted herself again and offered, "Do you want me to grab a new filter on my way home?"

Clawdeen's mom pushed her thick hair away from her face and squinted. "That would be great. Wait, what? Way home from where?"

"I'm going to go over to Draculaura's castle for the afternoon to get some quiet work time in before everyone arrives later." She smiled her most charming smile. "I promised Cleo and Draculaura I'd help them with their designs for the show. They finished their designs—and they look great!—but they want some help with the stitching. Okay?"

"No," her mom said, exasperated. "No, it's not okay."

"But, Mom," Clawdeen began, "Howleen's all up in my business here, and I just want to help my ghoulfriends and maybe get a few more pieces cut and stitched myself before"—she shrugged—"well, before the crazy hits."

"Clawdeen," her mom warned. "Our family is not crazy...."

"Crazy in a good way!" Clawdeen said quickly, before her mom could get really upset. Clawdeen smiled. "I love it when everyone comes to visit. The pack is clawesome; it's just...I want to take a few hours to get some work done before everyone gets here. Please?"

Her mom shook her head. "I'm sorry, but we can't spare you. We have so much cleaning to do, and I need your help this afternoon getting the food ready for our welcome feast tonight. Dad and Clawd are already out at the store getting steaks, and Howleen is working on getting your things moved so we have room for everyone to sleep."

Clawdeen held up a hand. "Howleen is doing *what*?" she screeched. "Nuh-uh, she is *not* moving my things."

"She certainly is. We need to make space for everyone to sleep."

Clawdeen said, "I'm happy to give up my room, but I need to move my own stuff. Who knows what Howleen's going to ruin while she noses around on my side of the room?!"

"Clawdeen…" her mom warned again. "We're all pitching in here. I asked your sister to help me get your room ready for Great-Great-Great-Gran and Great-Great-Great-Grandwolf. While the family is in town, you and your sister will be sleeping in the den with your cousins. I'm sorry you want to spend the afternoon with your friends, but you know the rules—the pack comes first. And I need help with dinner."

"The ghouls are part of my pack too!" Clawdeen growled. "Don't you realize how important it is that I help them with their designs for the show?"

Her mom lifted her eyebrows and gave Clawdeen a look.

"Fine," Clawdeen grumbled. "I'll just ditch my ghoulfriends and *cook* all afternoon."

"Wonderful," her mom said with a smile. "A wise choice."

Clawdeen turned and began to storm out of the room, her bag hanging, heavy with unfinished dresses, over her shoulder. Just as her mom opened the vacuum to try to clear out the filter again, Clawdeen spun around. She couldn't help herself. Sometimes it was impossible not to say what was on her mind. "Don't you realize how important this show is to me?" she asked. "I'm raising money for Monster High. It's a chance for me to prove to everyone that I have what it takes to do this on my own. That I can run my own business and manage a team and…" She broke off, feeling like she was speaking without being heard.

But her mom's expression softened, and she said, "Of course I know how important this show is to you, Clawdeen. But I also know how important family time is. I'm sorry this family reunion will make things difficult for you, but some things will need to be set aside for quality family time these next couple of weeks. You'll make it work. You always do."

Clawdeen groaned. That's almost exactly what her brother had said to her the day before. And it was just what she *didn't* need to hear. She already *knew* she could do it. She *had* to do it—once she had committed to something, Clawdeen Wolf wasn't the kind of ghoul who didn't get the job done. She was nothing if not absolutely confident about her own abilities—it wouldn't be easy, but she would figure out a way to get this show ready no matter what.

But that didn't mean she wasn't annoyed that her family didn't seem to understand just how much work it was to put together her own Freaky-Fabulous Fashion Show. And she wondered if they realized that this was more than just a fun hobby—it was her passion. Fashion design was her life. Did they know that?

Not for the first time in the past few years, Clawdeen longed to feel like her family understood that she had other things that mattered as much to her as the Wolf pack did.

Diary Entry

It felt clawesome to vent my frustrations to Clawd this afternoon. He and I spent most of the afternoon putting dinner together (getting food ready for thirty hungry werewolves is a serious project!), and we chatted about how the pack rules can be really hard to deal with sometimes. We both feel like our friends are part of our pack too, but I know that's not exactly acceptable to Mom and Dad and the grans and all our other relatives. Packs are supposed to be all wolf, but it's different for us. We both have several packs that are important to us, and it's hard to juggle them all.

The rest of our Wolf pack arrived about an hour ago, and things are already <u>CRAZY</u> around here. My little cousin Clawdette has more personality in one paw than some people have in their whole body. She's full of energy, bursting with drama, and always singing. (Except for the singing, she reminds me of a certain ghoul I know...me!) I love the pup, but I have a feeling sleep is going to be hard to come by this week. She's spent the past twenty minutes bouncing from the couch to a beanbag chair to the kitchen counter with the little quadruplets. Her feet haven't touched the ground once. (The quadruplets aren't as coordinated, so they keep rolling off everything, banging into all the furniture.) When I asked them what they were up to, Clawdette told me they're pretending that the floor is hot wax, and if any of them touch it, all their hair will get ripped off. Ha! I don't even know where she gets this stuff!

I'm still planning to sneak in some work time whenever I can. All my stuff was moved out of my room and pushed into a corner of the den, where I'm hoping it will be safe. I have seven pieces that are mostly finished, two more that are in a pretty good place, and four outfits that are just a heap of fabric right now. Cleo's been calling me almost hourly to talk about the dress she's working on, and Draculaura is desperate to come over to show me what she's done. Mom keeps barking at me to get off the phone, which is complicating everything big-time.

I haven't even begun to think about snacks and drinks we could serve before or after the show, and Frankie, Draculaura, and I haven't had any time to talk about stage and set design. I'm not usually the kind of ghoul who asks for help, but there's too much for a lone wolf to get done on her own. I'm so grateful for my ghoulfriends, who have stepped up to help.

I've read in my business magazines that keeping a checklist of what needs to be done is one way that some of the big executives keep organized, so I've decided to try it. Here's my checklist of what's still to be done:

- ☑ Finish sketches (Clawesome! One done!)
- ☐ Finish sewing
- ☐ Fit dresses to all models
- ☐ Help the ghouls with their designs
- ☐ Set design
- ☐ Snacks
- ☐ Drinks
- ☐ Figure out my own outfit for the show!

Okay, that's not at all scary. (Gulp!) I've got this, though. It's like a track meet—time to perform under pressure! I'm running for the finish line, and there's no way I'm not going to win.

NOTE: This is a <u>PRIVATE</u> diary. If I catch someone looking at these pages, REVENGE will be added to my to-do list. Consider yourself warned.

Clawdeen

CHAPTER
FOUR

"Clawdeen, your bed is very comfortable." Great-Great-Great-Gran wrapped her furry hand around Clawdeen's arm and gave it a comforting squeeze. "When I'm at home, I toss and turn and paw at my blankets to make a comfy spot before I can fall asleep. This afternoon, when I snuggled in for a nap on your bed, I fell asleep instantly. I'm very refreshed." She yawned, then patted Clawdeen's hand. "Thank you for giving up your room for Great-Great-Great-Grandwolf

56

and me for the next few weeks. I know how hard it can be for a teen wolf to give up her personal space. I used to be able to curl up and sleep any-where, but lately the floor just isn't as comfortable as it once was."

Clawdeen smiled at her great-great-great-gran and wrapped her into a warm hug. "I'm glad you're comfy here, Gran. And I'm more than happy to share my room with you. No way would I let you sleep on the floor!"

Great-Great-Great-Gran was the oldest of Clawdeen's relatives. But for someone who was hundreds of years old, she was still full of energy. Even still, Clawdeen would never consider asking one of her elders to sleep on the floor while she took a bed—it was unheard of! Every pup in the wolf clan had been taught early in life to be respectful to the wolves who had come before them, no matter what. Clawdeen leaned in and whispered, "By the way, you're lucky Grandwolf got stuck with Howleen's bed…who knows when she last changed her sheets!" Gran laughed her loud, barking laugh, and Clawdeen joined her.

One of the things Clawdeen loved most about all her grans was their clawesome sense of humor. The Wolf family loved teasing one another, and they all knew that any kind of joking around was done in good fun. Clawdeen curled up on the floor next to her gran's chair to chat. She hadn't seen her great-great-great-gran in several months, and they had a lot of catching up to do.

"Will you still be able to work on some of your sewing while we're here for a visit?" Gran asked, her warm voice quiet and scratchy. "Your mother tells me you've been working on some designs for a new fashion show?"

Clawdeen's face lit up. "I am!" She told her gran all about why she had decided to put together the Freaky-Fabulous Fashion Show, and how it was going to be her first solo show. She didn't tell her just how much she had left to do to get everything ready—it wasn't her style to burden someone else with her worries. Besides, she didn't want it to seem like she didn't have things under control. Suddenly, Clawdeen jumped up. "Would you like to see some of my designs, Gran?"

"Of course, dear. Is there anything that might fit me?" Gran asked with a wink. She patted her conservative blue slacks and sweater, and giggled. "I'd enjoy seeing how I look in some of the new fashions you pups are wearing these days."

Clawdeen helped her gran to her feet. "Of course! You're about the same size as my ghoul-friends at Monster High—except for maybe Draculaura, who is super petite! You'd look totally clawesome in aqua. Why don't you try on the outfit I designed for my friend Lagoona Blue? It's not completely done yet, but seeing it on someone will be really helpful for me as I finish the stitching and detail work."

Great-Great-Great-Gran shuffled across the room, following Clawdeen to a corner of the den. Clawdeen pulled back the sheet and revealed her rack of designs. Gran reached out and gently ran one of her long fingernails over all the fabrics, oohing and aahing over everything. Clawdeen swelled with pride. She loved to impress people with her work, and impressing someone who had seen as many things as Great-Great-Great-Gran had in her unlife was especially rewarding. "They all feel so expensive," Gran murmured.

"That's what's fabulous about designing and stitching your own clothes," Clawdeen told her as she carefully pulled Lagoona's outfit off the rack. "I can design pieces that are even better than the ones in the most expensive stores in the Maul, but they cost just a sliver of the price."

Clawdeen helped Great-Great-Great-Gran slip into Lagoona's ensemble for the show. Everyone was so busy talking and laughing and there was so much commotion around them that no one else in the family even noticed what they were up to. So it was a huge surprise to the whole pack when, a few minutes later, Great-Great-Great-Gran paraded through the den wearing a pair of fitted white pants with a flowing aqua top. Clawdeen had pulled her gran's hair back into a headband, Gran's shoes were off, and she was wearing a huge smile. The whole look made it seem like Gran was hundreds of years younger than she really was.

Gran strutted and sauntered past the rest of the family, laughing and bowing as everyone whistled and cheered her on. Clawdeen was howling with laughter by the time Gran made her way back to the rack in the corner, and Gran was wheezing from giggling so hard.

Clawdeen and Gran linked arms to take a bow. "I'm next," called Great-Gran. "I like red! You have anything on that rack that would fit me?"

"I'm a gold girl myself," called out one of Clawdeen's aunties.

"I don't like anything that's too tight!" hollered another. "Do you have anything flowy?"

Soon, everyone was calling out their style preferences, and Clawdeen was beginning to worry a little about how many people might want to try on her pieces. She loved sharing them, of course, but she didn't want to risk anything getting damaged before the show. Luckily, a moment later, Clawdeen's dad called everyone outside to dinner, giving Clawdeen a few minutes to herself to put everything away. She carefully hung the pieces back up and covered the entire rack with the protective sheet, tucking the corners in tightly and hoping the rack would stay that way.

As she made her way out to join her family, she thought about how much fun it was to share her work with the people she loved. She was happy she had a family who was so supportive of her talents, but she also wondered if they realized that part of being supportive was also giving her the time she needed to work. She didn't mind giving up her room for the week, but she was also worried about whether she'd be able to carve out a quiet spot to get her sewing done. Great-Great-Great-Gran had told her she could use her own room whenever she wanted—but Clawdeen knew that was true only when her great-great-great-gran and grandwolf weren't in there. And both of them napped several times a day, so there were limited windows of time when she could sneak away. The den would be filled with cousins all the time, so there was no hope of privacy there, either.

As she grabbed a plate and lifted a giant, deliciously rare steak off a platter in the middle of the table, Clawdeen tried not to worry about it. So she hadn't gotten a moment to work on the show all day—but it was just the first day of her family's visit. Things would be a little less hectic tomorrow...she hoped. Because even though Clawdeen loved hanging out with her pack, this surprise family reunion had major potential to seriously cramp her style!

Diary Entry

This family reunion is monstrously fun, but things have not slowed down at all since everyone arrived. It's usually totally clawesome having a huge pack around in the summer, as you can find someone who's up for tossing around a ball or going for a run or even getting a pickup baseball game going. (Right now we have enough people in this house to field three whole teams!)

Trouble is, I don't really have time to toss around a ball or go for a run. I've got <u>hours of work</u> to do... and I'm starting to miss my ghoulfriends! Family's great, but I need to get in some time with my other pack soon too!

But every time I've tried to slip away this week to get some work done, someone's grabbed me to ask questions about how school's going, talk about sports, or ask me for advice on their wardrobe. I know it would be rude to walk away—and I could never do that to my pack—but sometimes that's just what I want to do!

Yesterday, Cousin Clawdette bounced over and asked me when I'm going to be famous. She wants to see my name on a label inside her school sweaters so she can brag about me to her ghoulfriends. I know she means well, and it's sweet that she's so proud of me... but in the moment, I almost snapped and told her it wasn't going to happen anytime soon, since I haven't had more than a few minutes to work on my Freaky-Fabulous Fashion Show the whole time they've been staying with us. But luckily I didn't say that. I managed to take a deep breath and keep my fur from flying. It wasn't easy to hold my tongue.

My to-do list doesn't look much better. Note for next show: Leave <u>more time</u> to get everything done!

- ☑ Finish sketches
- ☑ Finish sewing (I'm checking this off even though I still have two pieces left to finish because I'm close enough that I can smell the finish line.)
- ☐ Fit dresses to all models (Can't do this until I can sneak away to see the ghouls... soon, I hope!)
- ☐ Help the ghouls with their designs
- ☐ Set design (The ghouls are on this. I sent them color ideas and a few sketches for what I'm thinking about. Draculaura's amazing at interior design, and Frankie is great at effects—I bet she and her dad will come up with some voltageous effects in their lab!
- ☐ Snacks

☐ Drinks

☐ Figure out my own outfit for the show!

NOTE: This is a PRIVATE diary. Hands off. You do NOT want to get on my bad side right now. Read this, and you'll face a fate worse than running out of conditioner. What's worse than a mane full of knots? You don't want to find out.

Clawdeen

CHAPTER FIVE

More than a week had passed since the Wolf family arrived at Clawdeen's house. Day after day was filled with eating, playing, laughing, and pack bonding. They were all having a blast, but still, Clawdeen thought that a week of family time had earned her and her siblings at least one night out with friends. Draculaura and her new stepmomster were throwing a start-of-summer party at Dracula's castle, and all the Wolf kids were eager to be there.

"So who's going to tell Mom and Dad we're going out?" Howleen asked, looking from Clawd to Clawdeen and back again. "I'm the youngest, so when I ask for things they always tell me I can do it when I'm older. So that leaves one of you."

Clawd and Clawdeen both yelped, "Not it!" at the same time.

"I said it first," Clawdeen insisted.

"Nuh-uh," Clawd said, laughing. "Ladies first!"

Clawdeen narrowed her eyes at him. "It's your ghoulfriend's party."

Clawd shrugged. "She's your beast friend. Besides, this was your idea."

"Fine," Clawdeen growled. "Be a pup. I'll do it."

"They're going to say no," Clawdia said. She looked up from the book she was reading and shrugged. Maybe it was because she was used to the hustle and bustle of Londoom, but Clawdia seemed to be especially good at tuning out distractions. She had spent much of the past week curled up in a chair in the den reading as the whole family scuttled around her. "You know pack comes first."

"What about our other packs?" Clawdeen insisted.

Clawdia shrugged again. "I'm just sayin'... they're going to say no."

"I'll work my magic," Clawdeen promised. "I know how to get what I want."

But a few minutes later, she returned to the den looking crestfallen.

"I take it your magic didn't work?" Clawd teased.

"Not at all," Clawdeen snapped. "In fact, I—"

Clawdeen was cut off when her dad stepped into the room. "Thanks again for agreeing to babysit, kids. It will be nice for us to go out to dinner with the adults and to give your aunties the night off." He left the room and then returned a moment later, snapping his fingers as if he had just remembered something. "Oh, and it's a full moon, so the little ones are a little rowdier...than usual. Good luck!"

Clawd, Clawdia, and Howleen stared at Clawdeen. She said, "I think I made it worse?"

The front door slammed. Suddenly, high-pitched yelping rang through the house. "Wooooo!" howled Cousin Clawdette. "The oldsters are gone! The house is *oouuuurs!*"

Clawdette came running past her older cousins with the quadruplets in tow. "Woooo!" she shrieked. "Wooooooo!"

Clawdeen looked at Clawdia with a pleading expression. Her older sister stuffed a pair of headphones in her ears and muttered, "This time at home is supposed to be my summer vacation. I took my turn babysitting when you were all pups. Now it's *your* turn."

"What are we supposed to do with them all night?" Howleen asked helplessly.

"You've been looking for a chance to prove to everyone just how mature you are," Clawdeen reminded her. "Here's your chance!"

"No way," Howleen said, shaking her head. "I'm not doing this alone."

"TV?" Clawdeen suggested. "Boo-vies?"

"You heard Dad," Howleen said. "They're all amped up because of the full moon. I'm feeling a little twitchy too.... There's no way they're going to sit through a boo-vie."

"Cooking?" Clawdeen asked. "These pups are always hungry."

Howleen gaped at her. "Who wants to clean up *that* mess?"

"Arts and crafts," Clawd said calmly. "What pup *doesn't* love arts and crafts?"

"You're a genius," Clawdeen said, hugging

him. "I think I have some stuff we could give them to design their own T-shirts!"

The three siblings split up to search the house for arts-and-crafts supplies. Meanwhile, their little cousins continued to run and jump and leap all through the house. Clawdeen was digging through a box of her sewing supplies when she heard something crash to the floor in the kitchen. Grabbing an armful of fabric, a few spare T-shirts, and some of her favorite glue-on embellishments, she ran toward the noise. "Who wants to do a project?" she said, poking her head into the den.

Her mouth fell open. Clawd came up behind her. "Uh-oh..."

Clawdeen struggled to keep herself from howling. For there, in the middle of the den, were all her cousins...wearing the pieces she'd designed for her Freaky-Fabulous Fashion Show.

"How do I look?" Clawdette asked. She spun around. The dress Clawdeen had designed for

Frankie was hanging loosely from her cousin's tiny frame. The quadruplets were each wearing an outfit of their own, and one of them had Draculaura's purse dangling from his ear. The few pieces that remained on the rack were torn and messy. Clawdeen could tell that she had a monstrous disaster on her hands.

She couldn't speak. Her whole body went numb. She dropped the supplies she'd been holding. The embellishments and glue and fabric all clattered to the ground. Clawdette and the quadruplets looked at the pile of crafting supplies excitedly.

With a shriek, Clawdette lunged forward and grabbed a bottle of fabric glue. Before Clawdeen even realized what was happening, her little cousin had trimmed a piece of glittery gold fabric into the shape of a crescent moon and glued it to the bottom of Frankie's dress for the fashion show. "Pretty," Clawdette said with a smile. "I love crescent moons. Don't you, Clawdeen?"

Clawdeen reached for her little cousin, but it was too late. The scrap of fabric moon was already glued in place. With only four days to go before the fashion show, Frankie's dress was ruined. Clawdeen sank to the floor and put her head in her paws. Her life—and every one of her designs—had gone from great to absolute disaster in no time at all.

Diary Entry

Arrrrrrrrrrrr!

I'm so <u>frustrated</u>. I love my little cousins like crazy but tonight made it a lot harder to like them. Somehow, they managed to destroy all my pieces for the show. Clawd and Howleen tried to tell me not every piece is <u>totally ruined</u>, but I can't even look at the destruction. I put so much work into each of those pieces, and it's going to be impossible to do it all over again in the time I have. I'm furious, sad, and frustrated...not a good combo!

While I was chasing her around the den, trying to get the little pup's furry paws off my dresses,

Clawdette managed to stick crescent moons on almost all the pieces for the show. Then the naughty little pup told me I should have a special signature— something to tell the world I designed each of the dresses. And because she likes crescent moons, she GLUED GLITTERY MOONS ON EVERYTHING.

Grrrrrrr!

I'm trying really hard to be a supportive member of the pack, but it's getting to be monstrously hard not to totally flip out. Moons? MOONS?

Hmmm.

Hold on.

You know what?

The pup might have a point.

A design element that runs through all my pieces isn't a terrible idea. And moons are, well, scary-cute. And my kitty cat is named Crescent, so they really do suit me.

Is there some way I can use Clawdette's, uh... alterations... to my advantage?

Something to consider.

Another thing I remember reading in one of my business blogs is that, as an entrepreneur, you must be able to deal with curveballs. Having my outfits destroyed less than a week before showtime is definitely a curveball. Now I just have to figure out how to deal with it.

List time again:

- ☑ Finish sketches
- ☐ Finish sewing (Thought I was done with this one... guess not)
- ☐ Fit dresses to all models
- ☐ Help the ghouls with their designs
- ☐ Set design (I guess this is super close to being done, but I haven't seen it yet. Control freak that I am, I want to see it with my own eyes. But I love my ghoulfriends for taking care of this for me!)
- ☐ Snacks

☐ Drinks

☐ Figure out my own outfit for the show!

NOTE: This is a PRIVATE diary. Hands off. You do NOT want to get on my bad side right now. Read this, and you'll face a fate worse than tofu. What's worse than tofu? You don't want to find out.

Clawdeen

CHAPTER SIX

The morning after the babysitting disaster, Clawdeen woke up feeling like she hadn't slept a wink. The truth was, she'd tossed and turned all night, dreams of her ruined creations flashing through her mind. She was determined to salvage her pieces and kept telling herself, "The show must go on," but it was hard to keep up the positive attitude because she was also steaming mad. By the time she and her siblings managed to pry their little cousins out of all the dresses the night before, the den was a disaster area. Fabric scraps littered the floor, strips of lace were strewn across the sofa, and messy little crescent-moon cutouts were *everywhere*. When the adults got home from dinner, they didn't even seem to notice the disaster in the den. That only added to Clawdeen's frustration.

Clawdeen stretched, rolled over, yawned…and came face-to-face with Clawdette. She was lying on the cushion right next to Clawdeen's, staring straight at her. Her little cousin looked sheepish. "I'm sorry we played dress-up with your stuff," she said quietly. Then, after a pause, she added, "It's just that you let Great-Great-Great-Gran try on one of your dresses, so I thought…" Tears welled up in her eyes, and she rolled over, her back to Clawdeen.

Clawdeen sighed, then reached out and rubbed her little cousin's shoulder. Clawdeen still wasn't happy, but she knew none of this was Clawdette's fault. She was just a little pup, and she'd been excited. When werewolves were under the influence of the full moon, their senses were heightened, and it could be hard to calm down. Neither her age nor the moon made what she'd done any less horrible, but realizing Clawdette hadn't done it to be mean made her much more forgivable.

"I get it," Clawdeen said. "I used to love dress-up when I was a pup. One time, I snuck into my mom's closet while she was cooking dinner and pulled everything off the hangers. Every stitch of clothing she had! I was too little to hang anything up again, but I didn't want to get in trouble for not cleaning up after myself. So I just stuffed it all back in the closet in a wrinkled heap. When she saw what a mess I'd made, my mom was furious."

Clawdeen laughed, remembering how much trouble she'd gotten into that day. But it had been worth it, trying on all her mom's clothes and shoes and posing in front of the mirror like a model. Then the whole family had pitched in to help iron everything and clean up the mess, and all was forgotten a little while later. It wouldn't be quite as easy to clean up Clawdette's mess, but it was kind of the same thing.

Clawdette giggled too. "You loved to play dress-up?"

"I still do," Clawdeen said. "That's probably why I love designing so much. I get to dress myself and my friends with the best dress-up clothes *ever*—the ones I created! How clawesome is that?"

Clawdette grinned and popped up and out of bed. "I'm hungry," she announced. "Let's get breakfast." Apparently, their chat was over. Clawdette had moved on. That was the great thing about pups—they could apologize for something and then move on. But Clawdeen wasn't going to be able to move past last night's mess quite as quickly. Her show was in three days, and every one of her pieces was ruined.

She pulled on some clothes, brushed her hair and teeth, then made her way toward the kitchen. Clawdeen really wasn't in the mood to see her family, but if she didn't come down for breakfast, she knew it would be seen as a sign of disrespect. As she passed the den, she couldn't keep her eyes from wandering over to her rack of designs in the corner. Her whole body rumbled with anger again. The sheet she had used to keep everything protected was torn and ragged, the dresses were all hanging messily from their hangers, and Clawdette's glittery crescent moons were still everywhere. If possible, it looked even worse to Clawdeen than it had the night before.

Clawdeen walked over and picked up a few of the pieces. She ran her fingers across the stitching, hems, and detail work. It was possible that some of the garments could be saved—with lots of repair work—but others were too destroyed and would have to be cut and sewn again. There was no way she could do everything on her list in less than three days.

The only good thing was that Clawdeen hadn't yet had a chance to pick up her friends' designs from them. She had planned to store all the show pieces in one spot, but because she hadn't seen her ghoulfriends since the day after school had let out for the howlidays, the other ghouls' designs were safe and sound at Draculaura's and Cleo's homes. The Freaky-Fabulous Fashion Show would go on...but not as many of Clawdeen's designs would be included. That meant fewer would be sold at the end of the show and they would earn less money for Monster High.

Growling, Clawdeen walked into the kitchen. No one even seemed to notice her. If one of Clawdeen's friends or siblings were upset, Clawdeen could always sense it right away. But there were so many people crowded into the kitchen that Clawdeen just blended in.

She stormed around, grabbing a coffincino and a plate of scrambled eggs and bacon from the counter. Everyone in the family was laughing and talking and going on with their business as if *nothing* at all had happened. Clawdeen's mood soured with each bite of her breakfast. Did no one understand just how much she had lost last night? Did anyone realize that her show was going to be a voltageous fail? Was *anyone* going to offer to help her get things back in order? It seemed not.

After breakfast, Clawdeen gathered up some of her sewing stuff and carved out a work space in the den to try to mend her designs. She longed for Draculaura's company—a ghoulfriend who could sit with her and maybe help stitch—because she understood how important this show was to Clawdeen. Instead, the only company she got was Clawdette—who kept popping out from behind a sofa to ask if she wanted a snack, then asking for Clawdeen's help finding one. Then the quadruplets asked if she would help them fill their soccer ball with air. Then one of the aunties asked for her help with the dishes. It was noon before Clawdeen could put her head down and get to work.

"Clawdeen?" her mom said, standing over her. Clawdeen had been working for ten minutes to try to remove glue residue from Frankie's dress.

"What?" she snapped.

Her mother lifted her eyebrows. "I was wondering if you want to come with us to get ice scream. Some of your aunties wanted to stop at the Maul afterward to do a little shopping, and they were hoping to get your help putting together some new outfits." Her mom cocked her head. "I thought you might enjoy that! What do you say? Can you come shoppping and help your aunties with their style?"

"What do I say?" Clawdeen said, pushing her Freaky-Fabulous Fashion Show pieces to the side. "Does it *look* like I have time to go shopping right now?"

"Clawdeen!" her father scolded, looking up from the card game he was playing with the grandwolves. "I don't like your tone."

"Neither do I," her mom added.

"And I don't like that my fashion show is ruined!" Clawdeen snapped. "But I have to deal with it." She jumped up, hollering, "I wish someone in this family would understand how much this show means to me. This is my chance to help earn money for the things that matter most to me at Monster High—and a chance to show everyone I can do this. My ghoulfriends have been giving up their time to help me get everything ready, and it seems like the only thing my family has done is get in my way! If you ask me, my ghoulfriends are acting more like my pack than any of you are!"

Clawdeen slammed her mouth closed. She knew she had gone too far. The whole house went silent, and dozens of glowing eyes were suddenly staring at her. She had never said anything so hurtful in her life. Clawdeen ran from the room—embarrassed, ashamed, and more frustrated than ever.

Diary Entry

It turns out that an afternoon with my ghoulfriends was just what I needed to relax. After I full-on freaked out at my family this afternoon, I knew the only way for me to cool off was to get out of the house. I had to step away, or I was afraid of what more I might say. So I left a note for Mom and Dad, told Clawd he better have my back, and went to Draculaura's to meet up with the other ghouls. Cleo and Draculaura showed their designs to me, and seeing their pieces—almost finished and GORE-GEOUS!—made me feel much better.

Even though I won't have more than a few of my designs ready for the show, at least we'll still have a show. A monstrously amazing show. The Freaky-Fabulous Fashion Show isn't going to be anything like I'd imagined it could be, but that's unlife. Sometimes, you've got to make the most of a hairy situation and figure out how to make it less tangled the next time.

After talking to the ghouls today, here's what I've realized: My family is <u>majorly important</u> to me and I do want to be loyal to the pack... but I wouldn't be the ghoul I am without my <u>ghoulfriends'</u> influence too. They've helped me figure out my strengths and develop my individual style over the past few years at Monster High. Getting together with them to talk, laugh, plan, and vent helps me feel like ME.

So even though my Freaky-Fabulous Fashion Show isn't going to be what I had originally hoped it would be, I'm ready to deal with it coolly and calmly. I'm going to make the most of it, Clawdeen-style. Three days to tick off the rest of the boxes. I'll do the best I can and make the most of what I've got! That's what a fierce fashionista does!

- ☑ Finish sketches
- ☐ Finish sewing
- ☐ Fit dresses to all models
- ☑ Help the ghouls with their designs
- ☑ Set design
- ☐ Snacks
- ☐ Drinks
- ☐ Figure out my own outfit for the show!

NOTE: No sniffing around my diary. Or my designs. Seriously. Fur will fly if anyone touches anything that belongs to me. I may have calmed down, but it's still a mostly full moon. So watch out!

Clawdeen

CHAPTER SEVEN

When Clawdeen returned from Draculaura's castle late that night, the whole Wolf pack was curled up watching a boo-vie together in the den. Clawdeen slipped past the piles of fur, grabbed her sewing kit, and settled in on the floor to get to work on her repairs while she listened to the boo-vie in the background. It was one of the Werewolf Dynasty movies, and Clawdeen knew most of it by heart.

Clawdeen's family loved watching werewolf

movies together. They would all laugh and growl at the TV, howling about the silly story lines, but Clawdeen knew they all secretly thought they were pretty great.

By the time the boo-vie ended, Clawdeen had nearly finished the repairs on the dresses she had made for Frankie and Draculaura to wear in the show. She had also traced out her pattern for Lagoona's outfit, which she needed to start from scratch, since it had been damaged, and she had cut the fabric so she could start over on Cleo's gown first thing in the morning. Once she'd had a chance to take a closer look, Clawdeen was relieved to see that the red dress from her collection was in good shape (though it still smelled like Howleen). There was a ton to do on the rest of her pieces, but there was no way she would get it all done in the time she had left. She went to bed exhausted and disappointed, but more determined than ever.

When she woke up a few hours later, she immediately got back to work. The house was quiet, and she was able to get more than an hour of work in before the frenzy of breakfast began.

"Clawdeen?" Just as Clawdeen began to hear the house coming awake with the sounds of morning, Clawd poked his head up over her makeshift workstation. He held out a coffincino and grinned. "You joining us for breakfast?"

"Oh," she said, taking a sip of the hot coffee before biting off a piece of thread with her teeth. "Um…" She looked at her pile of work, feeling the same rush of tension and motivation. She had to succeed. She *had* to.

"Listen," Clawd said. "Everyone feels bad about what happened yesterday. I think you'd feel better too if you came to breakfast and apologized." Clawdeen began to say something, but Clawd held up a hand to stop her. "You and I both know you said some mean stuff. You feel bad, I can tell. I also know it's hard that the family doesn't always seem to get you, but that doesn't mean you should direct your anger at them. What happened with Clawdette was an accident—she's just a pup—and it's no one else's fault."

"I know that." Clawdeen sighed. "It's just... well, it just seems like no one cares how much work I've put into this. And after everything was torn to shreds the other night, not one member of the pack even offered to help me!"

Clawd folded his arms across his chest. "Have you *asked* for help?"

"No," Clawdeen snapped.

"Well, maybe you should start there and see where it gets you." Clawd lifted his furry eyebrows. "I know you're fiercely independent, but sometimes, sis, it's okay to ask for help. When there are this many people around, it can be hard to see when someone is struggling. Maybe, if you told the family what you need their help with, you'd see just how much they *do* support you. Give them a chance." With that advice, Clawd turned and headed back to the kitchen.

Clawdeen suddenly realized Clawd was right. All week, her family had been asking for her help when they needed a hand with something—the dishes, fashion advice, cooking, whatever. But she hadn't even *tried* asking them for help. She had just gotten frustrated with them for getting in her way. Maybe if she had included them on the preparations for her show—the way she had trusted and included her ghoulfriends to step in and help out—things would have gone much smoother from the start. Feeling more positive than she had in days, Clawdeen gulped down her coffincino and bounded into the kitchen, where her entire pack was enjoying breakfast.

"Listen up," Clawdeen said, clapping her hands to get everyone's attention. "I need to apologize for what I said yesterday. I never should have snapped at all of you. It was out of line, and I'm sorry. I love you all, and I hope you know that."

The pack surrounded her, offering up hugs and reassurances and pats on the back. "Of course we know that, sweetie," said her mom.

"I'm proud of you for apologizing," her dad said as he looped an arm around her shoulder and gave her a squeeze.

"We love you too, Clawdeen," said Clawdia. "Always and forever."

Clawdette stepped forward and held up a clump of fabric that had been roughly cut and sewn into the shape of a sack dress. "I have something for you, Cousin Clawdeen," she said. "I made a new dress for your show, since I ruined some of the other ones. I wanted to help."

Clawdeen held up the lumpy mess of fabric and smiled. "It's scary-cute, Clawdette. You're a budding designer!" She looked to the rest of her family and said, "I should have asked sooner, but ... would the rest of you be willing to help me too? I could really use a few extra paws."

There was a chorus of yeses. "Of course! We would be happy to help with your show," said one of her aunties.

"That's what a pack does," added Great-Great-Great-Gran. "We help out when someone asks for it. You're an independent ghoul, Clawdeen. We didn't think you *wanted* our help."

Clawdeen breathed a sigh of relief. "Well, if I'm going to get the rest of this show put together in the next two days, I could definitely use a lot of help from everyone—all of you guys *and* my Monster High ghoulfriends." She glanced at her parents, then let her gaze wander to her gran. "Is that okay? Could I invite some of the ghouls over to help me too? With help from my *whole* pack—my family and my friends—I bet I can get everything done and then some."

The Wolf elders looked at one another, and unspoken words passed among them. Finally, Great-Great-Great-Gran nodded. "I realize the world is different for you than it was for me, Clawdeen. Though I don't always understand it, if your...uh, ghoulfriends"—she cleared her throat—"are what you need to fulfill this dream of yours to make your fashion show come to unlife, then we wouldn't want to stand in the way of that. We want you to be happy."

Clawdeen rushed forward and gave her great-great-great-gran a huge hug. "Thank you," she whispered.

Less than an hour later, Draculaura, Lagoona, Cleo, and Frankie had joined the Wolf pack at Clawdeen's house. Everyone was ready to pitch in to turn Clawdeen's freaky fashion disaster around.

Like a true leader, Clawdeen gave everyone a job to do. Her aunties were busy cutting the remaining patterns. Great-Great-Great-Gran and Great-Great-Great-Grandwolf, Clawdeen's mom, and Cleo proved to be best at stitching. (Though Cleo mostly put her feet up and watched the others work, pointing out whenever they made mistakes. Clawdeen had to admit, Cleo always excelled at giving orders.) Clawd, Howleen, Clawdeen's dad, and Lagoona were working with the quadruplets to whip up some delicious snacks they could serve at the show. Frankie was working on concocting a fun fruit punch that would change colors throughout the night. And Clawdette, Clawdeen, Draculaura, and Clawdia worked together on the final details of each of Clawdeen's designs. Slowly but surely, the last items on Clawdeen's to-do list were checked off.

"I hope you don't mind," Clawdeen said, winking at her little cousin, "but I've decided to take an idea you had and use it for the show."

"One of my ideas?" Clawdette asked. She gazed up at Clawdeen, her big eyes filled with surprise.

Clawdeen held up Frankie's dress. It was finally finished, and after the repair work Clawdeen had done, it was even better than it had been *before* the babysitting snafu. She spun the fabric around in her arms, pointing out the detailed design running across the bottom of the dress. The original version of the dress had just used plain lace detailing on the gown. Now it was much more special and unique. Clawdeen grinned at her cousin and said, "See?"

"They're moons!" Clawdette gasped, looking down at the dress. "The bottom is decorated with golden crescent moons made out of lace! You used my moons!"

"I've decided to incorporate a crescent moon somewhere on each of my pieces for the show," Clawdeen explained. "You were right—I need a signature for my designs. And I think it makes a lot of sense for my signature to reflect my scaritage. And it's even more special because I got the idea from you!"

Clawdette jumped up and down, nearly knocking over the rack of finished dresses. But before she crashed into it, Clawdia reached out and grabbed her arm to steady her. Clawdeen's big sister winked at her, then said to Clawdette, "Let's go see if we can taste test some of the fashion show snacks while Clawdeen finishes up here, shall we?"

Clawdette and Clawdia ran off to get a snack in the kitchen, leaving Clawdeen and Draculaura alone for a moment. "Are you feeling a teensy bit better about your Freaky-Fabulous Fashion Show now?" Draculaura asked. "Everything looks totes amazing."

"I *feel* amazing," Clawdeen said. "About *our* show. I couldn't have done any of this without all of you. It's not my show anymore—it's all of ours! And it's so much better because of how many people helped out."

"Think we'll be ready in time?" Draculaura said, smiling.

"I *know* we'll be ready." Clawdeen surveyed the rack of finished dresses in front of her. Working together, Clawdeen's pack had cut, assembled, stitched, and finished every one of her original designs for the show—including Clawd's suit, Howleen's skirt and top, and dresses for a bunch of the other Monster High ghouls who would be joining them for the show.

After a ton of false starts, Clawdeen was almost done with her own dress for the Freaky-Fabulous Fashion Show too. It was the softest, most elegant gown she had ever designed for herself. It was constructed out of rich gold satin, with delicate black stitching running through the whole bodice. The neckline of the dress was fur-lined, and there was a tiny crescent moon cut out right at the deepest point of the neckline. She looked like a boo-vie star—or the head of a fabulous fashion empire!—when she put it on.

Though Clawdeen knew there was a monstrous amount of stuff left to do the next day—rehearsals, setup, sound and light checks—she suddenly realized she had a few more outfits she needed to design. If this show were going to represent Clawdeen, there was a little more work that still had to be done.

Diary Entry

It's showtime! I can't believe we finished everything in time. It looks clawesome, if I do say so myself! I couldn't have done this without the help of my pack. Here's what we've managed to pull together in the last few weeks (and most of it was done in the last few days!):

- ☑ Finish sketches
- ☑ Finish sewing (twice!)
- ☑ Fit dresses to all models (including my NEW pack of models!)
- ☑ Help the ghouls with their designs

- [x] Set design
- [x] Snacks
- [x] Drinks
- [x] Figure out my own outfit for the show! (Draculaura told me it looks totes amazing, and I've got to agree. This is one of my best pieces ever!)

I haven't slept in more than twenty-four hours, but all the extra work was worth it! I loved seeing the looks on my family's faces when I told them I wanted some of them to walk alongside my Monster High pack in the Freaky-Fabulous Fashion Show. Over the past day, I designed and sewed special outfits for my mom, gran, great-gran, great-great-gran, and of course great-great-great-gran to wear on the runway. And what fashion show would be complete without a guest appearance from Clawdette and the dress she designed all on her own? She's already told me she plans to cartwheel down the runway. Who am I to stop her? She's expressing herself in her own freaky-fabulous way, and I love it!

Each of my models looks creeperific. The pieces all turned out so much better than I could have hoped, and each of the ghouls' own designs is a fun complement to my signature style. We work so well together!

Clawd and Deuce have spent the whole day strutting around in their fangulous outfits, acting like they're real models. I think they feel special that there are only two guys in the show. I just hope they can strut their stuff on the runway too! I'm not holding my breath. Note for next time: I guess I need to work on more manster designs—I tend to be more of a dress and scary-cute-skirt ghoul myself, but it would be good to expand my design skills to include more clothes for the guys.

I know there are plenty of things I can learn from this experience for next time, but I'm really proud of what I put together (freaky flaws and all). This show doesn't just represent my mix of fashion styles—it also represents Monster High and my own big blended pack perfectly!

I've already heard from a bunch of people—including one of the head buyers at Neiman Monstrous!—who want to buy dresses from me after the show. And there are more than two hundred people lined up outside to come in. We're going to make a ton of money for Monster High, and I couldn't be happier.

It feels amazing to know that I've done just what I set out to do: create a Freaky-Fabulous Fashion Show that is a true representation of who I am. I couldn't be prouder of the show or of my packs. That's right, I said "packs": my Wolf pack and my pack of ghoulfriends.

Clawdeen

Start your own clawesome diary, just like Clawdeen! On the following pages, write about your own creepy-cool thoughts, hopes, or screams...whatever you want! These pages are for your eyes only! (Unless you want to share what you write with your ghoulfriends!)

MONSTER HIGH

Here's a sneak peek inside the diary
of another fangtastic friend,
Draculaura...

MONSTER HIGH
DIARIES

DRACULAURA
AND THE NEW
STEPMOMSTER

Nessi Monstrata

Diary Entry

You are totes not going to believe this...my dad is getting married! Another vampire caught his eye at the Ice Ball in Antarctica last year. He saw her across the room, asked her to dance, and was sucked in. Just like that! Isn't it the scary-cutest story ever?

I don't think there is anything sweeter than love at first bite.

Dad's trying to play it cool. (You know Father. Always so serious!) But from what he's told me, Ramoanah (that's her name!) is just amazing and he's totes into her. After that night at the ball, they spent the next few months chilling out in Antarctica, and now

THEY ARE GETTING MARRIED!

I ♡ weddings!

But here's my tiny, little, itsy-bitsy secret. (Just a teensy thing. No big deal, I'm sure.) I'm kinda freaking out. I don't actually know much about Ramoanah. Since she and Dad have been away in Antarctica and I've been here—attending Monster High— I haven't even met her. And she's going to be my stepmomster in less than a week!

I'm sure she's going to be fangtastic, just like Dad says she is. How could she not be? Still, I'm a little nervous, you know? What if she...

Ugh! I can't even write it!

What if she...doesn't like me?

I know, I know. That would be silly. We'll probably be beast friends, right? We'll share style tips and watch boo-vies together. Maybe it will be so fangtastic having her around that it will be hard to even remember that it's been just Dad and me for the past 1,600 years.

I can't wait for the wedding—it's going to be so <u>glamorous</u> and elegant! And I'm so excited for my ghoulfriends to see what a real Transylvanian vampire wedding is like. They will all get to learn more about my vampire scaritage. The ghouls can meet my family and a ton of old vamp friends. Here's the best part: We all get to stay at the Chateau Transylvania (it's the fanciest hotel EVER—even Cleo will be impressed!).

Oh, and I have a feeling that I might get to be <u>Ramoanah's maid of horror!!</u> Or at least a batsmaid (that would be totally ghoul too). I'm hoping she will ask me as soon as we meet....I want to be prepared, so I'm going to buy the most fangtastic hot pink and black dress ever created. I was so thrilled when Dad told me that Ramoanah had chosen black and pink as the colors for the wedding—looks like she and I have the same fave colors! I can't wait to help her with all the final wedding plans when we get to Transylvania tomorrow!

Gotta go! More soon.

Smooches,
Draculaura

CHAPTER ONE

"What do you think, ghouls?" A sweet and cheerful vampire named Draculaura stepped out of the changeling room at Neiman Monstrous, her favorite store in the Maul. She spun in circles. A shimmering, lacy black dress with beautiful hot pink details swirled around her legs. The dress matched her black-and-pink-streaked hair perfectly and made her pale pink skin glow. "Is this the one?"

"Gore-geous," Clawdeen Wolf proclaimed as she stopped pawing through racks of dresses to check out her ghoulfriend. Clawdeen was a fierce and stylish werewolf with a nose for fashion. "It's perfect."

Frankie Stein's one green and one blue eye went wide. "That pink makes you look totally voltageous, Draculaura." Frankie, the only daughter of Frankenstein, also had a scary-cute style all her own, though she loved just about anything with black-and-white stripes.

"I think we have a winner." Draculaura giggled. Then she slipped behind the curtain to change back into her school clothes. "Don't you just love weddings?" she called as she carefully pulled off the dress. "I can't believe my *dad* is the one getting married!"

"You haven't been to a wedding until you've been to a royal wedding," Cleo de Nile announced. Cleo—a mummy and Egyptian princess who was as loyal of a friend as she was a pampered diva—

was sprawled out on a sofa nearby, impatiently waiting for the glass of fresh-squeezed orange juice she had insisted the shop clerk bring her to sip on while she waited for her friend to choose a dress for Dracula's wedding. "Oh, but I'm sure your dad's wedding will be really great too...."

"It's going to be totally amazing, Draculaura!" Clawdeen agreed excitedly. "I'm stoked that us ghouls all get to come along. I never thought a werewolf like me would be taking *two* trips to Transylvania so close together."

Draculaura stepped out of the changeling room. "I'm excited too, ghouls. I feel so lucky that I get to have my beast ghoulfriends there with me. I just wish everyone at Monster High could come!" She sighed. "Because of course, the one little thing that would make this weekend extra fangulous would be having Clawd along. I'm going to miss my sweetie so much. Going to Dad's wedding without him totally bites."

"No way," Clawdeen replied quickly, shaking one sharp fingernail at her beast friend. The last thing she wanted was one of her siblings tagging along on the trip of this lifetime. Her pack stuck together too much as it was—sometimes, she just wanted to be with her beasties. "This weekend it's just us ghouls. And it's going to be clawesome!"

Their zombie friend, Ghoulia Yelps, grunted her agreement. Ghoulia blinked behind her horn-rimmed glasses and readjusted the headband in her long, thick blue hair. She tucked the book she had been reading into her purse for later.

Cleo rolled her eyes playfully and yawned. "If we ever leave the Maul, that is. Are you almost done, Draculaura? I think I aged another year while we waited for you to pick something."

"Ready!" Draculaura said cheerfully. She knew Cleo was only teasing—after all, Cleo was a stylish mummy who enjoyed shopping as much as any other ghoul!

The Neiman Monstrous clerk—a slow-moving zombie—grunted as she lurched toward the counter to ring up Draculaura's purchase.

"I love that it's just going to be us ghouls too but...I don't get why Clawd *can't* come along," Frankie said.

Draculaura frowned as she replayed in her head the conversation she'd had with her dad. Her father had been acting sort of weird in the days leading up to the wedding. Ever since he'd called to tell Draculaura about his fiancée, he had been acting even more serious than usual. Draculaura was pretty sure it was just prewedding jitters. But she was still a little hurt about what he had said when she asked for permission to invite Clawd. She told her friends, "My dad thought Ramoanah's family might have a hard time swallowing the fact that I'm dating a non-vampire. Vampires, werewolves...you know. We're not exactly known for getting along."

"Well, we'll just have to help change their minds about that!" said Clawdeen.

"I'm sure everything will be fine," Draculaura said quickly. She hoped Clawdeen was right...but deep down she worried that it might not be so easy. "My dad is always super welcoming to other monsters. I'm sure Ramoanah will be too. Her relatives are probably just a little more conservative than Dad and I are. As you ghouls know, some vampires can have a teensy, eensy problem with anyone who isn't a vampire...so I think Dad just wants to play it safe."

"Some old, stuffy vampires like Lord Stoker," sniffed Clawdeen, thinking about her last trip to Transylvania with Draculaura. Lord Stoker had tried to make Draculaura believe she was the long-lost vampire queen. Luckily, Draculaura and her ghoulfriends figured out that Lord Stoker was tricking her, along with the rest of the vampires, so he could continue to control the vampire court. Draculaura and the Monster High crew had managed to find the *real* vampire queen—Draculaura's old friend Elissabat—and made Lord Stoker look like a fool.

"Exactly." Draculaura giggled. "There are still a lot of vampires like Lord Stoker in Transylvania. The kind who think vampires should be the most respected and feared monsters in the world." She rolled her eyes at the silliness of it all.

"Ugh," groaned Cleo. "That is so last century. Besides, it's obvious that if any monsters were to be the most respected in the world, it would be the de Niles." Cleo smiled at her beast friend and asked, "Isn't that right, Ghoulia?"

Ghoulia patted Cleo's arm and smiled. Sometimes, it was easiest just to agree with Cleo. Ghoulia knew her beast friend had pretty strong opinions and really loved when people agreed with her.

As they strolled out of Neiman Monstrous, Frankie said, "I bet the food is going to be totally electric!" She grinned as she imagined the fancy new foods she would get to try. "And speaking of food...Ramoanah's family knows you're a vegetarian, though, right, Draculaura?"

Draculaura cringed. Unlike every other vampire she had ever met, she didn't drink blood—she preferred fruits and veggies and lots of protein supplements. Just the thought of blood made her queasy, and she had been known to faint at the mere mention of the word!

Draculaura and her dad had discussed her vegetarianism a lot over the years—it was hard for her dad to understand how Draculaura could be so different from other vamps. But deep down, she knew Dracula respected her choice. "I don't know if they know..." she said, her voice trailing off uncertainly. "I mean, I'm sure my dad must have told Ramoanah, but I don't know if she told her family or not. I hardly know anything about Ramoanah, actually. The only thing I know for sure is that my dad is batty about her and that she's going to be a part of my family. I'm going to have to spend a lot of time getting to know her before the wedding!" She tried to smile, but her deepest worries about having a new stepmomster were rearing their ugly heads in her mind, and that made it almost impossible to pull off a real smile.

Her ghoulfriends could all sense something was wrong. Ghoulia asked Draculaura what was eating her.

"It's nothing," squeaked Draculaura.

"Come on," prodded Frankie. "You can tell us. We're your beast friends."

Draculaura clutched the dress bag in her arms. She knew that telling her ghoulfriends what she was worried about would probably make her feel much better. "It's just that…even if Ramoanah's great—which I'm sure she will be!—I'm sort of nervous about everything changing."

"I get it," said Clawdeen. "It's been just you and your dad together for the past sixteen hundred years. It's definitely going to be different having a stepmomster around."

"But it's going to be great," added Frankie.

"You think?" asked Draculaura. "I just don't know how we're going to fit someone new into our family after all this time. And what if my dad likes her more than he likes me? Or what if Ramoanah doesn't like me? What if things change, and..."

"Things will change. That's unlife," Cleo said firmly. "But the other stuff you're worrying about is totally ridiculous," she added in a softer voice. She placed a hand on Draculaura's shoulder to comfort her. "Your dad loves you. That's never going to change."

The other girls nodded. Ghoulia said, "Everyone adores you, Draculaura. You're such a true ghoulfriend."*

---

* *Translated from Zombese*

"Ghoulia's right," said Clawdeen. "Everyone loves you. And your dad has room for both of you in his life. Ramoanah is going to adore you too."

Frankie hugged her friend. "No one could ever take your place in your dad's heart."

"Thanks, ghouls," Draculaura said with a smile. "You're the beast." After talking through her concerns with her ghoulfriends, she certainly felt much better. They were right. She was probably worrying for no reason.

They had a fangtastic wedding weekend to look forward to. She wasn't going to waste a moment of it worrying. She grinned and linked arms with her ghoulfriends. "We leave tomorrow, so you know what that means—just a few hours to find the perfect wedding shoes!"

And just like that, all of Draculaura's worries about meeting Ramoanah floated away as she and her ghouls hunted for the most perfectly fangtastic shoes in the Maul.

Diary Entry

I LOVE monster High to the max, BUT there is something so exciting about visiting Transylvania. I just love getting to reconnect with my vampire scaritage. It brings back so many fangulous memories of growing up in the vampire court. Sometimes it feels like forever ago that Dad and I fled Transylvania for the Boo World.

Just between you and me, it was hard for me to leave Transylvania. I missed my friends, the pretty mountains, and all that lovely purplish night sky. It sure did help that Dad had our whole house rebuilt in the Boo World. So even though unlife is super different now than it was when we lived in Transylvania, the Boo World feels like home.

And of course, I've met so many creeperific monsters at Monster High that I can't even imagine going back to the old life. I would never have met Frankie, and Clawdeen, and Cleo, and Ghoulia, and Lagoona, and CLAWD, and...well, you get my point.

Sometimes I forget that Frankie hasn't seen much of the world yet. She was totes adorable when we boarded the train for Transylvania today. She got so electrified about the trip that she began to spark, and all the lights in the train went out! That poor ghoul...she just can't help but get excited about new adventures.

And speaking of being excited, my sweet little pet bat, Count Fabulous, is going batty too! He loves the Boo World, but I can tell he is happy we are going back to Transylvania! Well, gotta fly! More later.

Smooches,
Draculaura

Did you 🖤 reading Clawdeen's diary?
Then you will also love reading
CLEO DE NILE'S DIARY...
COMING SOON!